Good Manufacturing Practices (GMP) Modules for Pharmaceutical Products

Good Manufacturing Practices (GMP) Modules for Pharmaceutical Products

Chandrasekhar Panda

ISBN 978-93-5458-305-6
© Chandrasekhar Panda 2021
Published in India 2021 by Pencil

A brand of

One Point Six Technologies Pvt. Ltd.
123, Building J2, Shram Seva Premises,
Wadala Truck Terminal, Wadala (E)
Mumbai 400037, Maharashtra, INDIA
E connect@thepencilapp.com
W www.thepencilapp.com

DISCLAIMER: *The opinions expressed in this book are those of the authors and do not purport to reflect the views of the Publisher.*

Author biography

The author of this Topic is Chandrasekhar panda who is having more than 14 years of Experience in Pharmaceutical Quality Assurance department and he has worked in Pharma Companies like Cipla, USV & Aurobindo Pharma Limited.

CONTENTS

Good Manufacturing Practices (GMP) Modules for Pharmaceutical Products

<u>What is Good Manufacturing practices (GMP) :</u>

Good manufacturing practice (GMP) is a system for ensuring that products are consistently produced and controlled according to quality standards. It is designed to minimize the risks involved in any pharmaceutical production that cannot be eliminated through testing the final product.

The main risks are:

Unexpected contamination of products, causing damage to health or even death; incorrect labels on containers, which could mean that patients receive the wrong medicine; insufficient or too much active ingredient, resulting in ineffective treatment or adverse effects.

GMP covers all aspects of production; from the starting materials, premises and equipment to the training and personal hygiene of staff. Detailed, written procedures are essential for each process that could affect the quality of the finished product. There must be systems to provide documented proof that correct procedures are consistently followed at each step in the manufacturing process - every time a product is made.

<u>What is Current Good Manufacturing practices</u>

(cGMP) :

The letter "c" stands for "current," reminding manufacturers that they must employ technologies and systems that are up-to-date in order to comply with the regulation.

Can Manufacturers afford to implement GMP:

Yes. Making poor quality products does not save money. In the long run, it is more expensive finding mistakes after they have been made than preventing them in the first place. GMP is designed to ensure that mistakes do not occur. Implementation of GMP is an investment in good quality medicines. This will improve the health of the individual patient and the community, as well as benefiting the pharmaceutical industry and health professionals. Making and distributing poor quality medicines leads to loss of credibility for everyone: both public and private health care and the manufacturer.

There are various Modules of GMP which are required for Pharmaceutical products which includes GMP for plant premises, Equipment's, Production, Training, personnel Hygiene, Qualification & Validation, Quality Management system, Self-Inspection, quality audits and suppliers' audit, Personnel, Quality Control, and Complaints & Recall.

Module-1   Pharmaceutical   Plant   Premises Requirement as Per GMP

Below given details are the GMP requirements for the Pharmaceutical Plant premises or campus and Premises or campus must be located, designed, constructed, adapted and maintained to afford the Operations to be carried out.

General Requirements :

The layout and design of premises must aim to minimize the risk of errors and permit effective cleaning and maintenance in order to avoid cross contamination, build-up of dust or dirt, and in general, any adverse effect on the quality of products.

Where dust is generated (e.g. during sifting, weighing, mixing and processing operations, or packaging of powder), measures should be taken to avoid cross-contamination and facilitate cleaning.

Premises used for the manufacture of finished products should be suitably designed and constructed to facilitate good sanitation.

Premises should be carefully maintained, and it should be ensured that repair and maintenance operations do not present any hazard to the quality of products.

Premises should be cleaned and, where applicable, disinfected according to detailed written procedures and records should be maintained.

Electrical supply, lighting, temperature, humidity and ventilation should be appropriate and such that they do not adversely affect, directly or indirectly, either the pharmaceutical products during their manufacture and storage, or the accurate functioning of equipment.

Premises should be designed and equipped so as to afford maximum protection against the entry of insects, birds or other animals. There should be a procedure for rodent and pest control. Premises should be designed to ensure the logical flow of materials and personnel movement.

Additional Areas :

Rest and refreshment rooms should be separate from manufacturing and control areas.

Facilities for changing and storing clothes and for washing and toilet purposes should be easily accessible and appropriate for the number of users and Toilets should not communicate directly with production or storage areas. Maintenance workshops should if possible be separated from production areas. Whenever parts and tools are stored in the production area, they should be kept in rooms or lockers reserved for that use.

Storage Areas :

Storage areas should be of sufficient capacity to allow orderly storage of the various categories of materials and products with proper separation and segregation which includes starting and packaging materials, intermediates, bulk and finished products, products in quarantine, and released, rejected, returned or recalled products.

Storage areas should be designed or adapted to ensure good storage conditions. In particular, they should be clean, dry, sufficiently lit and maintained within acceptable temperature & Relative humidity limits. Where special storage conditions are required (e.g. temperature, humidity) these should be provided, controlled, monitored and recorded where appropriate.

Receiving and dispatch bays should be separated and should protect materials and products from the weather. Receiving areas should be designed and equipped to allow containers of incoming materials to be cleaned, if necessary, before storage.

Where quarantine status is ensured by storage in separate areas, these areas must be clearly marked and their access restricted to authorized personnel.

Segregation should be provided for the storage of rejected, recalled, or returned materials or products.

Highly active and radioactive materials, narcotics, other dangerous medicines, and substances presenting special risks of abuse, fire or explosion should be stored in safe and secure areas.

Printed packaging materials and similar looking packing materials are considered critical to the pharmaceutical product hence its labeling and special attention should be taken to safe and secure storage of these materials.

There should normally be a separate sampling area for starting materials. (If sampling is performed in the storage area, it should be conducted insuch a way as to prevent contamination or cross-contamination.)

Weighing Areas :

The weighing of raw material, intermediate, or a drug substance should be carried out in separate weighing areas designed for that use, for example, with provisions for dust control. Such areas may be part of either storage or production areas.

Production Areas :

In order to minimize the risk of a serious medical hazard due to cross contamination, dedicated and self-contained facilities must be available for the production of particular pharmaceutical products, such as highly sensitizing materials (e.g. penicillin's) or biological preparations (e.g. live microorganisms). The production of certain other highly active products, such as some antibiotics, hormones, cytotoxic substances and certain non-pharmaceutical products should not be conducted in the same facilities. In exceptional cases, the principle of campaign working in the same facilities can be accepted provided that specific precautions are taken and the necessary validations (including cleaning validation) are made. The manufacture of technical poisons, such as pesticides and herbicides, should not be allowed in premises used for the manufacture of pharmaceutical products.

Premises should preferably be laid out in such a way as to allow the production to take place in areas connected in a logical order corresponding to the sequence of the operations and to the requisite cleanliness levels.

The adequacy of the working and in-process storage space should permit the orderly and logical positioning of equipment and materials so as to minimize the risk of confusion between different pharmaceutical products or their components, to avoid cross-contamination, and to minimize the risk of omission or wrong application of any of the manufacturing or control steps.

Where starting and primary packaging materials and intermediate or bulk products are exposed to the environment, interior surfaces (walls, floors and ceilings) should be smooth and free from cracks and open joints, should not shed particulate matter, and should permit easy and effective cleaning and disinfection.

Pipework, light fittings, ventilation points and other services should be designed and sited to avoid the creation of recesses that are difficult to clean. As far as possible, for maintenance purposes, they should be accessible from outside the manufacturing areas.

Drains should be of adequate size and designed and equipped to prevent back-flow. Open channels should be avoided where possible, but if they are necessary they should be shallow to facilitate cleaning and disinfection.

Production areas should be effectively ventilated, with air-control facilities (including filtration of air to a sufficient level to prevent contamination and cross-contamination, as well as control of temperature and humidity where necessary) appropriate to the products handled. These areas should be regularly monitored during both production and non-production periods to ensure compliance with their design specifications.

Premises for the packaging of pharmaceutical products should be specifically designed and laid out so as to avoid mix ups, contamination or cross-contamination.

Production areas should be well lit, particularly where visual online controls are carried out.

Quality control Areas :

QC laboratories should be separated from production areas. Areas where biological, microbiological or radioisotope test methods are employed should be separated from each other.

QC laboratories should be designed to suit the operations to be carried out and sufficient space should be given to avoid mix ups and cross contamination.

There should be adequate suitable storage space for samples, reference standards (if necessary, with cooling), solvents, reagents and records.

The design of the laboratories should take into account the suitability of construction materials, prevention of fumes, and ventilation. There should be separate air supply to laboratories and production areas. Separate air-handling units and other provisions are needed for biological, microbiological and radioisotope laboratories.

A separate room may be needed for instruments to protect them against electrical interference, vibration, contact with excessive moisture and other external factors, or where it is necessary to isolate the instruments.

<u>Module-2   Pharmaceutical   Plant   Equipment's Requirement as Per GMP</u>

Equipment's must be located, designed, constructed, adapted and maintained to suit the operations to be carried out. The layout and design of equipment must aim to minimize the risk of errors and permit effective cleaning and maintenance in order to avoid cross-contamination, build-up of dust or dirt, and any adverse effect on the quality of products.

Equipment should be installed in such a way as to minimize any risk of error or of contamination.

Equipment should be Qualified before use i.e. Design, Installation, operational and Performance Qualification of the equipment's shall be completed before use.

Fixed pipework should be clearly labeled to indicate the contents and, where applicable, the direction of flow i.e. purified water, Potable water and Compressed Air etc.

All service pipework and devices should be adequately marked and special attention paid to the provision of non-interchangeable connections or adaptors for dangerous gases and liquids.

Balances and other measuring equipment of an appropriate range and precision should be available for production and control operations and should be calibrated according to a fixed schedule i.e. Calibration and daily Verification of weighing balances, Calibration of In process checks instruments like Disintegration tester, Friability, LOD apparatus, Vernier caliper, Hardness and Thickness Tester, leak test apparatus .

Production equipment should be thoroughly cleaned according to a fixed schedule or after product to product change over or batch to batch change over or based upon validity of Cleaned equipment or Dirty equipment's.

The cleaning, usage and preventive maintenance details shall be mentioned in the respective equipment logbooks separately which shall content Date, Product name, Batch number, cleaning or usage activity start time, End time, activity done by, checked by and type of cleaning or preventive maintenance etc.

Production equipment should not present any hazard to the products. The parts of the production equipment that come into contact with the product must not be reactive, additive, or absorptive to an extent that would affect the quality of the product.

Material of construction of the equipment's contact part should be Stainless Steel 302, 304, 304L, 316, 316L and Teflon etc.

Defective equipment should be removed from production and QC areas. If this is not possible, it should be clearly labeled as defective to prevent use.

A periodic preventive maintenance schedule shall be prepared for each equipment's and after each preventive maintenance equipment's shall be cleaned.

Closed equipment should be used whenever appropriate. Where open equipment is used or equipment is opened, precautions should be taken to minimize contamination.

Non-dedicated equipment should be cleaned according to validated cleaning procedures between being used for production of different pharmaceutical products to prevent cross-contamination.

Current drawings of critical equipment and support systems should be maintained.

Module-3 Pharmaceutical Plant Production Requirement as Per GMP

General Requirements :

The handling of materials and products, such as receipt, quarantine, sampling, storage, labeling, dispensing, processing, packaging and cleaning should be done in accordance with written procedures or instructions (Standard Operating Procedure) and, where necessary, recorded.

Deviation from instructions or procedures should be avoided as far as possible and if deviations occur, they should be in accordance with an approved procedure. The deviation shall be raised and approved and the required Corrective and Preventive action shall be taken.

What is Deviation :

Any unwanted event that represents a departure from approved processes or procedures or instruction or specification or established standard or from what is required. Deviations can occur during manufacturing, packing, sampling and testing of drug products.

Examples of Deviations:

Temperature and RH of area goes out of limit during manufacturing, Typographical error observed in approved documents, Standard operating procedure not followed, Breakdown of equipment, Spillage of material during unloading, Instrument calibration results goes out of limit etc.

Critical deviation:

A Critical Deviation is an unplanned event that affects a quality attributes a critical process parameter, an equipment or instrument critical for process control and has an immediate patient safety risk, life threatening situations.

Major deviation:

A Major Deviation is an unplanned event that potentially affects a product's quality, safety or efficacy or its ability to meet specification, or regulatory or documentation requirements which may not have direct impact on patient.

Minor deviation:

A Minor deviation is an unplanned event that potentially has GMP impact (e.g. an event affecting a utility, equipment, materials, components environment or documentation) but does not affect product quality and / or the physical state of the product, intermediate or component, or its labeling.

Yields and reconciliation of quantities should be carried out at different stages of Manufacturing and packing to ensure that there are no discrepancies outside acceptable limits.

Operations on different products should not be carried out simultaneously in the same room or area as there are the chances of mix up or cross-contamination.

During manufacturing and packing the major items of equipment's, the rooms, packaging lines being used should be labelled or otherwise identified with an indication of the product or material being processed. The labelled should contain Material name or product name, Batch number, Stage of manufacturing, done by, checked by and date etc. to avoid mix-up.

Access to production premises should be restricted to authorized personnel.

In-process controls are usually performed within the production area.

<u>Prevention of cross-contamination and bacterial contamination during production :</u>

When dry materials and products are used in production, special precautions should be taken to prevent the generation and spreading of dust. Provision should be made for proper air control (e.g. supply and extraction of air and dust extraction system).

Contamination of a starting material or of a product by another material or product must be avoided.

Cross-contamination should be avoided by taking appropriate technical or organizational measures, for example:

(a) carrying out production in dedicated and self-contained areas (which may be required for products such as penicillin's, live vaccines, live bacterial preparations and certain other biologicals);

(b) conducting campaign production (separation in time) followed by appropriate cleaning in accordance with a validated cleaning procedure;

(c) providing appropriately designed airlocks, pressure differentials, and air supply and extraction systems;

(d) minimizing the risk of contamination caused by recirculation or reentry of untreated or insufficiently treated air;

(e) wearing protective clothing where products or materials are handled;

(f) using cleaning and decontamination procedures of known effectiveness;

(g) using a "closed system" in production;

(h) testing for residues;

(i) using cleanliness status labels on equipment.

Measures to prevent cross-contamination and their effectiveness should be checked periodically according to SOPs. Production areas where products are processed should undergo periodic environmental monitoring (e.g. for microbiological and particulate matter, where appropriate).

Processing or Manufacturing operations :

Before any processing operation is started, steps should be taken to ensure that the work area and equipment are clean and free from any starting materials, products, product residues, labels and documents which are not required for the current operation.

Line clearance should be taken before starting of any activity for the respective areas and equipment's where batch processing shall be carried out.

What is Line Clearance :

Line clearance is a process which provides a high degree of confidence or assurance that the said line or area is free from any unwanted residue or left over of previous processing's before proceeding for next process. Quality assurance has to provide Line clearance before the start of any activity whether it is batch to batch change over and Product to product change over

Criteria of Batch to batch change over :

Change over from one batch to another batch of same product and same Strength or increasing in strength provided the excipients are same.

Cleaning between batches of same product but in ascending or increasing strength.

Criteria of Product to Product change over :

Change over from one product to another product.

Change over form one product to same product with descending or decreasing strength.

Change over between batches / product with different colour/ Flavor / Excipients.

Change over after post maintenance or when the next product is not known (as applicable).

Continuously running of one batch for a longer period of time.

Area or Equipment is kept ideal for more period of time.

Line clearance should be carried out at change over by Manufacturing, Packaging, and Raw Material Store, Packing Material Store etc. independently for the stages where final dosage form & intermediates are formed, handled and processed.

Any necessary in-process checks and environmental controls should be carried out and recorded during activity and at regular intervals.

Defective equipment should be withdrawn from use until the defect has been rectified. After use, production equipment should be cleaned without delay according to detailed written procedures and stored under clean and dry conditions in a separate area or in a manner that will prevent contamination.

Production equipment should be thoroughly cleaned according to a fixed schedule or after product to product change over or batch to batch change over or based upon validity of Cleaned equipment or Dirty equipment's.

Balances and other measuring equipment of an appropriate range and precision should be available for production and control operations and should be calibrated according to a fixed schedule i.e. Calibration and daily Verification of weighing balances, Calibration of In process checks instruments like Disintegration tester, Friability, LOD apparatus, Vernier caliper, Hardness and Thickness Tester, leak test apparatus .

The cleaning, usage and preventive maintenance details shall be mentioned in the respective equipment logbooks separately which shall content Date, Product name, Batch number, cleaning or usage activity start time, End time, activity done by, checked by and type of cleaning or preventive maintenance etc. Any significant deviation from the expected yield should be recorded and investigated.

Pipework, light fittings, ventilation points and other services should be designed and sited to avoid the creation of recesses that are difficult to clean. As far as possible, for maintenance purposes, they should be accessible from outside the manufacturing areas.

Water sampling should be done at a regular interval or as per scheduled in production area

Measuring, weighing, recording, and control equipment and instruments should be serviced and calibrated at pre specified intervals and records maintained. To ensure satisfactory functioning, instruments should be checked daily or prior to use for performing analytical tests. The date of calibration and servicing and the date when recalibration is due should be clearly indicated on a label attached to the instrument.

Repair and maintenance operations should not present any hazard to the quality of the products.

Packaging operations :

When the packaging is going to start particular attention should be given to minimizing the risk of cross-contamination and mix ups. Different products should not be packaged in close proximity unless there is physical segregation or an alternative system that will provide equal assurance.

Before packaging operations are begun, steps should be taken to ensure that the work area, packaging lines, printing machines and other equipment are clean and free from any products, materials or documents used previously and which are not required for the current operation. The line clearance should be performed according to an appropriate procedure and checklist, and recorded.

The name and batch number of the product being handled should be displayed at each packaging station or line.

Normally, filling and sealing should be followed as quickly as possible by labeling. If labeling is delayed, appropriate procedures should be applied to ensure that no mix ups or mislabeling can occur.

The correct performance of any printing (e.g. of code numbers or expiry dates) done separately or in the course of the packaging should be checked and recorded. Attention should be paid to printing by hand, which should be rechecked at regular intervals.

Before start of packing activity the Specimen proof like Foil carton, leaflet, label etc should be checked by both production and Quality assurance and same shall be preserved along with batch record Regular online control of the product during packaging should include at a minimum checks on:

(a) the general appearance of the packages;

(b) whether the packages are complete;

(c) whether the correct products and packaging materials are used;

(d) whether any overprinting is correct;

(e) the correct functioning of line monitors. Samples taken away from the packaging line should not be returned.

Any significant or unusual discrepancy observed during reconciliation of the amount of bulk product and printed packaging materials and the number of units produced should be investigated and recorded before batch release to market.

Upon completion of a packaging operation, any unused batch-coded packaging materials should be destroyed and the destruction recorded.

The excess printed packing materials like Aluminum foil, PVC/PVDC can be returned to warehouse with material return note.

Production records should be reviewed as part of the approval process of batch release and any deviation or failure of a batch to meet production specifications should be thoroughly investigated. The investigation should, if necessary, extend to other batches of the same product and other products that may have been associated with the specific failure or discrepancy.

Module-4 Pharmaceutical Plant Personnel Requirements as Per GMP

General :

For maintaining a satisfactory Quality system and control of pharmaceutical products depends upon people. For this reason there must be sufficient qualified personnel to carry out all the tasks for which the manufacturer is responsible. Individual responsibilities should be clearly defined and understood by the persons concerned and shall be recorded.

The manufacturer should have an adequate number of personnel with the necessary qualifications and practical experience.

Responsible personnel duties should be assigned based up on Experience and qualifications. The manufacturer or the company should have an organization chart.

All personnel should be aware of the principles of GMP and during joining they have to take the GMP training, personnel hygiene instruction, Good Documentation practice and Data Integrity etc. All personnel should be motivated to support the establishment and maintenance of high quality standards.

Steps should be taken to prevent unauthorized people from entering production, storage and QC areas. Personnel who do not work in these areas should not use them as a passageway.

Key Personnel :

Key personnel include the heads of production, the head(s) of quality unit(s) and the authorized person. The quality unit(s) typically comprises the quality assurance and

quality control functions. In some cases, these could be combined in one department. The authorized person may also be responsible for one or more of these quality unit(s). Normally, key posts should be occupied by full-time personnel. The heads of production and quality unit(s) should be independent of each other. Key personnel responsible for supervising the production and quality unit(s) for pharmaceutical products should possess the qualifications of a scientific education and practical experience required by national legislation. Their education should include the study of an appropriate combination of:
(a) Chemistry (analytical or organic) or biochemistry;
(b) Chemical engineering;
 (c) Microbiology;
(d) Pharmaceutical sciences and technology;
 (e) pharmacology and toxicology;
 (f) Other related sciences. They should also have adequate practical experience in the manufacture and QA of pharmaceutical products.

The heads of the production and the quality unit(s) generally have some shared, or jointly exercised, responsibilities relating to quality. These may include, depending on national regulations:
 (a) Authorization of written procedures and other documents
 (b) Monitoring and control of the manufacturing environment
 (c) Plant hygiene
 (d) Process validation and calibration of analytical apparatus
 (e) Training, including the application and principles of

QA;

(f) Designation and monitoring of storage conditions for materials and products;

(g) Performance and evaluation of in-process controls;

(h) Retention of records;

(i) Monitoring of compliance with GMP requirements;

(j) Inspection, investigation and taking of samples in order to monitor factors that may affect product quality.

Responsibilities of Head Production:

The head of production generally has the following responsibilities:

(a) To ensure that products are produced and stored in accordance with the appropriate documentation in order to obtain the required quality;

(b) To approve the instructions relating to production operations, including the in-process controls, and to ensure their strict implementation;

(c) To ensure that the production records are evaluated and signed by a designated person;

(d) To check the maintenance of the department, premises and equipment;

(e) To ensure that the appropriate process validations and calibrations of control equipment are performed and recorded and the reports made available;

(f) To ensure that the required initial and continuing training of production personnel is carried out and adapted according to need.

Responsibilities of Head Quality:

The head(s) of the quality unit(s) generally have the following responsibilities:

(a) To approve or reject starting materials, packaging materials, and intermediate, bulk and finished products in relation to their specifications;

(b) To evaluate batch records;

(c) To ensure that all necessary testing is carried out;

(d) To approve sampling instructions, specifications, test methods and other QC procedures;

(e) To approve and monitor analyses carried out under contract;

(f) To check the maintenance of the department, premises and equipment;

(g) To ensure that the appropriate validations, including those of analytical procedures, and calibrations of control equipment are carried out;

(h) To ensure that the required initial and continuing training of quality unit personnel is carried out and adapted according to need;

(i) Establishment, implementation and maintenance of the quality system;

(j) Supervision of the regular internal audits or self-inspections;

(k) Participation in external audit (vendor audit);

(l) Participation in validation programmes.

The authorized person is responsible for compliance with technical or regulatory requirements related to the quality of finished products and the approval of the release of the finished product for sale or supply.

Assessment of finished products should accept all relevant factors, including the production conditions, the results of in-process testing, the manufacturing (including packaging) documentation, compliance with the specification for the finished product, and an examination of the finished pack.

No batch of product is to be released for sale or supply prior to certification by the authorized person(s). In certain countries, by law, the batch release is a task of the authorized person from production together with the authorized person from QC.

The function of the approval of the release of a finished batch or a product can be delegated to a designated person with appropriate qualifications and experience who will release the product in accordance with an approved procedure. This is normally done by QA by means of batch review.

Module-5 Pharmaceutical Plant Training, Documentation and Personnel Hygiene Requirements as Per GMP

Training:

Training is the main aspects of Good Manufacturing practices and whenever a person joins in an organization he/she required to take the training which includes GMP, Good Documentation practices (GDP) and job related training etc.

What is Document:

A piece of written, printed, or electronic matter that provides information or evidence or proof of any activity that serves as an official record.

Why Good Documents are Required in Pharmaceuticals :

1. If it isn't documented, it didn't happen & we document to provide written proof that something happened.

2. For regulatory requirements & business reasons- intent of making quality product or cost saving improvements.

3.To Compliance with the Food and Drug

Administration's (FDA), Good Laboratory Practices, regulations (21 CFR Part 58), as well as GMP (Good Manufacturing practices) regulations for drugs and medical devices (21 CFR Parts 211 and 820) requires the use of Good Documentation Practices.

4. Good Documentation Practices (GDP) apply to everyone who documents activities related to cGMP (Current Good Manufacturing practices).

5. A key to Good Documentation Practices is to consider these questions each time you record your raw data:

a. is it true?   c.   Is it timely?

b. is it accurate?   d.   Is it legible?

The Organization should provide training with a written programme for all personnel those who are going to work in Production, Quality Assurance, Quality control, Engineering and warehouse departments (including the technical, maintenance and cleaning personnel).

Instructions to be followed for Good Documentation Practices (GDP) in Pharmaceuticals :

Write what you do, do what is written

Document shall be made clearly, readable, legible, accurate, prompt & consistent with water proof, nonfadable writing instrument, so that information cannot be erased or changed & easy to understand.

All documents / data should be written, signed and dated with permanent ink pen.

Date shall be written on the documents in the pattern of DD/MM/YY or DD/MM/YYYY & For the time, use 24 hours clock. No AM or PM shall be used. Time format shall be as HH:MM and wherever applicable time format shall be as HH:MM:SS.

Any mistake while recording the data during operation

should not be corrected with "Whitener", "Eraser" and "Overwriting" on the same.

In such case the wrong word is to be cancelled with horizontal cut line or striking-off the single line (i.e. Wrong) and rewrite the correct word with ink pen.

After cancellation and necessary correction the concerned person should put the valuable reason (if applicable) with signature and date. The reasons such as entry error, calculation error, printing error, transcription error, typographical error etc. can be used as applicable and as suitable. If sufficient space is not available for writing the reason, correction shall be numbered sequentially from 01 and the same shall be described at bottom of respective page by concerned person with signature and date.

Document entries should be done only by authorized person for that operation & don't use pencil for writing the documents / data.

Where the Ink Jet / Ribbon / any other Printer are used for presenting the data (Computer generated Report), the printing must be dark, clear, readable All computer generated reports must be reviewed, signed and dated.

Preferably, documents shall be prepared on "A4" size paper i.e. for Batch Manufacturing Record (BMR) and Batch Packaging Record (BPR), Analytical Work Sheet, Qualification Documents, Validation Protocols, or other cGMP Documentation.

Photocopy of any document without stamp shall be considered as "Uncontrolled Document".

Use of thermal paper for printing / documentation is to be avoided. Wherever required for printout, clear photocopy duly signed and dated shall be attached.

"Ditto Marks" (----"-------) shall not be used for

documentation.

"Bracketing" shall not be done for documentation.

In case issued document requires entry of additional data, information / addition of text matter which is not provided in the document, same shall be written legibly and shall be initiated by the person making the entry.

Whenever more than one option is available, encircle / tick the option which one is applicable. e.g. Batch Manufacturing Record, Analytical Worksheet etc.

Different types of the training are there which includes Induction Training, on job Training, Self Reading Training, External training and Refresher Training etc.

Training shall be conducted as per training Standard Operating Procedure (SOP) of the respective organization.

What is Standard Operating Procedure :

It is an authorized written document which describes the step by step instructions requirements for Quality system, performing operations, nonspecific to any product, process or material. It provides detailed procedure about systems applicable to various operation e.g. Equipment's / Instrument's / System's Operation / Cleaning / Maintenance.

Everybody working in organization has to follow the instruction which are written in SOP and perform their activities accordingly.

Importance of SOP :

It is important for all industry as it explains about the Practices & procedures which are to be followed by each department before doing any activity. It plays a major role in every business of an organization & it is the backbone of all industries and integral part of Quality Assurance.

Besides basic training on the theory and practice of GMP, newly recruited personnel should take training accordingly to their job responsibilities assigned to them. Training should also be given at a regular interval and as per scheduled and its practical effectiveness to be assessed periodically.

After completion of required training evaluation shall be done and based on evaluation the person can be eligible to perform his/her job responsibility and training record required to be maintained. Personnel working in areas where contamination is a hazard, e.g. clean areas or areas where highly active, toxic, Hormones, infectious or sensitizing materials are handled, should be given specific training i.e. Entry and Exit to production area, Uses of Personnel protective Equipment's and personnel hygiene etc.

Visitors or untrained personnel should preferably not be taken into the production and QC areas. If this is unavoidable, they should be given relevant information in advance (particularly about personal hygiene) and the prescribed protective clothing. They should be closely supervised by the plant personnel.

Consultant and contract staff or casuals should be qualified or trained for the services they provide. Evidence of this should be included in the training records.

Documents Required :
Labels

Labels applied to containers, equipment or premises should be clear, unambiguous and in the company's agreed format. It is often helpful in addition to the wording on the labels to use colours to indicate status (e.g. quarantined, accepted, rejected, and clean).

All finished medicines should be identified by labeling, as required by the national legislation, bearing at least the following information:

a) the name of the medicines;

(b) A list of the active ingredients (if applicable, with the INN), showing the amount of each present and a statement of the net contents (e.g. number of dosage units, weight, and volume);

(c) The batch number assigned by the manufacturer;

(d) The expiry date in an uncoded form;

(e) Any special storage conditions or handling precautions that may be necessary;

(f) Directions for use, and warnings and precautions that may be necessary;

(g) The name and address of the manufacturer or the company or the person responsible for placing the product on the market.

For reference standards, the label and/or accompanying document should indicate potency or concentration, date of manufacture, expiry date, date the closure is first opened, storage conditions and control number, as appropriate.

Batch processing records

A batch processing record should be kept for each batch processed. It should be based on the relevant parts of the currently approved specifications on the record.

The method of preparation of such records should be designed to avoid errors.
(Copying or validated computer programs are recommended. Transcribing from approved documents should be avoided.)

Before any processing begins a check should be made that the equipment and work station are clear of previous products, documents, or materials not required for the planned process, and that the equipment is clean and suitable for use. This check should be recorded.

During processing, the following information should be recorded at the time each action is taken, and after completion the record should be dated and signed by the person responsible for the processing operations:

(a) The name of the product;
(b) The number of the batch being manufactured;
(c) Dates and times of commencement, of significant intermediate stages, and of completion of production;
(d) The name of the person responsible for each stage of production;
(e) The initials of the operator(s) of different significant steps of production and, where appropriate, of the person(s) who checked each of these operations (e.g. weighing);
(f) The batch number and/or analytical control number and the quantity of each starting material actually weighed (including the batch number and amount of any recovered or reprocessed material added);

(g) Any relevant processing operation or event and the major equipment used;

(h) The in-process controls performed, the initials of the person(s) carrying them out, and the results obtained;

(i) The amount of product obtained at different and pertinent stages of manufacture (yield), together with comments or explanations for significant deviations from the expected yield;

(j) Notes on special problems including details, with signed authorization.

Batch packaging records

A batch packaging record should be kept for each batch or part batch processed. It should be based on the relevant parts of the approved packaging instructions, and the method of preparing such records should be designed to avoid errors. (Copying or validated computer programs are recommended. Transcribing from approved documents should be avoided.)

Before any packaging operation begins, checks should be made that the equipment and work station are clear of previous products, documents or materials not required for the planned packaging operations, and that equipment is clean and suitable for use. These checks should be recorded.

The following information should be recorded at the time each action is taken, and the date and the person responsible should be clearly identified by signature or electronic password:

(a) the name of the product, the batch number and the

quantity of bulk product to be packed, as well as the batch number and the planned quantity of finished product that will be obtained, the quantity actually obtained and the reconciliation;

(b) The date(s) and time(s) of the packaging operations;

(c) The name of the responsible person carrying out the packaging operation;

(d) The initials of the operators of the different significant steps;

(e) The checks made for identity and conformity with the packaging instructions, including the results of in-process controls;

(f) details of the packaging operations carried out, including references to equipment and the packaging lines used, and, when necessary, the instructions for keeping the product if it is unpacked or a record of returning product that has not been packaged to the storage area;

(g) whenever possible, samples of the printed packaging materials used, including specimens bearing the approval for the printing of and regular check (where appropriate) of the batch number, expiry date, and any additional overprinting;

(h) Notes on any special problems, including details of any deviation
from the packaging instructions, with written authorization by an appropriate person;

(i) The quantities and reference number or identification of all printed packaging materials and bulk product issued, used, destroyed or returned to stock and the quantities of product obtained to permit an adequate reconciliation.

There should be SOPs and records for the receipt of each

delivery of starting material and primary and printed packaging material.

The records of the receipts should include:
(a) The name of the material on the delivery note and the containers;
(b) The "in-house" name and/or code of material if different from (a);
(c) The date of receipt;
(d) The supplier's name and, if possible, manufacturer's name;
(e) The manufacturer's batch or reference number;
(f) The total quantity, and number of containers received;
(g) The batch number assigned after receipt;
(h) Any relevant comment (e.g. state of the containers).

There should be SOPs for the internal labeling, quarantine and storage of starting materials, packaging materials and other materials, as appropriate.

SOPs should be available for each instrument and piece of equipment (e.g.use, calibration, cleaning, maintenance) and placed in close proximity to the equipment.
There should be SOPs for sampling, which specify the person(s) authorized to take samples.
The sampling instructions should include:
(a) The method of sampling and the sampling plan;
(b) The equipment to be used;
(c) Any precautions to be observed to avoid contamination of the material or any deterioration in its quality;
(d) The amount(s) of sample(s) to be taken;
(e) Instructions for any required subdivision of the sample;

(f) The type of sample container(s) to be used, and whether they are for aseptic sampling or for normal sampling, and labeling;

(g) Any specific precautions to be observed, especially in regard to the sampling of sterile or noxious material.

There should be an SOP describing the details of the batch (lot) numbering system, with the objective of ensuring that each batch of intermediate, bulk or finished product is identified with a specific batch number.

The SOPs for batch numbering that are applied to the processing stage and to the respective packaging stage should be related to each other.

The SOP for batch numbering should ensure that the same batch numbers will not be used repeatedly; this applies also to reprocessing.

Batch-number allocation should be immediately recorded, e.g. in a logbook. The record should include at least the date of allocation, product identity and size of batch.

There should be written procedures for testing materials and products at different stages of manufacture, describing the methods and equipment to be used. The tests performed should be recorded.

Analysis records should include at least the following data:

(a) The name of the material or product and, where applicable, dosage form;

(b) The batch number and, where appropriate, the manufacturer and/ or supplier;

(c) References to the relevant specifications and testing procedures;

(d) Test results, including observations and calculations,

and reference to any specifications (limits);

(e) Date and reference number(s) of testing;

(f) The initials of the persons who performed the testing;

(g) The date and initials of the persons who verified the testing and the calculations, where appropriate;

(h) A clear statement of release or rejection (or other status decision) and the dated signature of the designated responsible person.

Written release and rejection procedures should be available for materials and products, and in particular for the release for sale of the finished product by an authorized person.

Records should be maintained of the distribution of each batch of a product in order, for example, to facilitate the recall of the batch if necessary.

Records should be kept for major and critical equipment, as appropriate, of any validations, calibrations, maintenance, cleaning or repair operations, including dates and the identity of the people who carried out these operations.

The use of major and critical equipment and the areas where products have been processed should be appropriately recorded in chronological order.

There should be written procedures assigning responsibility for cleaning and sanitation and describing in sufficient detail the cleaning schedules, methods, equipment and materials to be used and facilities and equipment to be cleaned. Such written procedures should be followed.

Personal Hygiene:
All personnel should undergo health examinations prior to

and during employment.

Personnel conducting visual inspections should also undergo periodic eye examinations.

All personnel should be trained in the practices of personal hygiene. A high level of personal hygiene should be observed by all those concerned with manufacturing and packing processes. Personnel should be instructed to wash their hands before entering production areas.

Any person shown at any time to have an apparent illness or open lesions that may adversely affect the quality of products should not be allowed to handle starting materials, packaging materials, in-process materials or medicines until the condition is no longer judged to be a risk.

All employees should be instructed and encouraged to report to their immediate supervisor any conditions (relating to plant, equipment or personnel) that they consider may adversely affect the products.

Direct contact should be avoided between the operator's hands and starting materials, primary packaging materials and intermediate or bulk product.

To ensure protection of the product from contamination, personnel should wear clean body coverings appropriate to the duties they perform, including appropriate hair covering. Used clothes, if reusable, should be stored in separate closed containers until properly laundered and if necessary, disinfected or sterilized.

Smoking, eating, drinking, chewing, and keeping plants, food, drink, smoking material and personal medicines should not be permitted in production, laboratory and storage areas, or in any other areas where they might adversely influence product quality. Personal hygiene procedures, including the wearing of protective clothing, should apply to all persons entering production areas, whether they are temporary or full-time employees or non-employees, e.g. contractors' employees, visitors, senior managers and inspectors.

Module-6 Pharmaceutical Plant Quality Control Requirements as Per GMP

General :

QC is the part of GMP concerned with sampling and testing of products and no materials should be used without testing or released. QC is not confined to laboratory operations, but may be involved in many decisions concerning the quality of the product.

Each manufacturer should have a QC function. The QC function should be independent of other departments and under the authority of a person with appropriate qualifications and experience. The basic requirements for QC are as follows:

(a) adequate facilities, trained personnel and approved procedures must be available for sampling, inspecting, and testing starting materials, packaging materials, and intermediate, bulk, and finished products, and where appropriate for monitoring environmental conditions for GMP purposes;

(b) To perform qualification and validation;

(c) Records must be made (manually and/or by recording instruments) demonstrating that all the required sampling, inspecting and testing procedures have actually been carried out and any deviations observed to be recorded and investigated;

(d) Records must be made of the results of inspecting and

testing the materials and intermediate, bulk and finished products against specifications

(e) Sufficient samples of starting materials and products must be collected to permit future examination of the product if necessary.

Other Responsibilities of Quality Control :

Other QC responsibilities include:

(a) Establishing, validating and implementing all QC procedures;

(b) Evaluating, maintaining and storing reference standards for substances;

(c) Ensuring the correct labelling of containers of materials and products

(d) Ensuring that the stability of the active pharmaceutical ingredients and products is monitored;

(e) Participating in the investigation of complaints related to the quality of the product;

(f) Participating in environmental monitoring;

QC personnel must have access to production areas for sampling and investigation as or whenever required.

All tests should follow the instructions given in the relevant written test procedure for each material or product. The result should be checked by the supervisor before the material or product is released or rejected.

Sampling should be carried out so as to avoid contamination or other adverse effects on quality. The containers that have been sampled should be marked accordingly and carefully resealed after sampling.

Care should be taken during sampling to guard against contamination or mix up of, or by, the material being sampled. All sampling equipment that comes into contact with the material should be clean.

Sampling equipment should be cleaned and, if necessary, sterilized before and after each use and stored separately from other laboratory equipment.

Each sample container should bear a label indicating:

(a) The name of the sampled material;

(b) The batch or lot number;

(c) The number of the container from which the sample has been taken;

(d) The number of the sample;

(e) The signature of the person who has taken the sample;

(f) The date of sampling.

Out-of-specification results obtained during testing of materials or products should be investigated in accordance with an approved procedure. Records should be maintained.

Before releasing a starting or packaging material for use, the QC manager should ensure that the materials have been tested for conformity with specifications.

Each batch (lot) of printed packaging materials must be examined following receipt.

Finished products:

For each batch of medicines, there should be an appropriate laboratory determination of satisfactory conformity to its finished product specification prior to release. Products failing to meet the established specifications or any other relevant quality criteria should be rejected.

Quality Control Record Review :

QC records should be reviewed which is a part of the

approval process of batch release before transfer to the authorized person. Any deviation or failure of a batch to meet its specifications should be thoroughly investigated. The investigation should, if necessary, extend to other batches of the same product and other products that may have been associated with the specific failure or discrepancy.

A written record of the investigation should be made and should include the conclusion and follow-up action. Retention samples or Control Samples from each batch of finished product should be kept for at least one year after the expiry date. Finished products should usually be kept in their final packaging and stored under the recommended conditions.

Samples of active starting materials should be retained for at least one year beyond the expiry date of the corresponding finished product. Other starting materials (other than solvents, gases and water) should be retained for a minimum of two years if their stability allows. Retention samples of materials and products should be collected in duplicate of double to perform reanalysis if required.

Stability studies :

QC should evaluate the quality and stability of finished pharmaceutical products and, when necessary, of starting materials and intermediate products.

A written programme for ongoing stability determination should be developed and implemented to include elements such as:

(a) A complete description of the medicine involved in the study;

(b) The complete set of testing parameters and methods, describing all tests for potency, purity, and physical characteristics and documented evidence that these tests indicate stability;

(c) Provision for the inclusion of a sufficient number of batches;

(d) The testing schedule for each medicine;

(e) Provision for special storage conditions;

(f) Provision for adequate sample retention;

(g) A summary of all the data generated, including the evaluation and the conclusions of the study. Stability should be determined prior to marketing and following any significant changes, for example, in processes, equipment or packaging materials.

Module-7 Qualification and Validation Requirements as Per GMP

Principle:

Qualification and validation are applicable to the facilities, equipment, utilities and processes used for the manufacture of medicinal products.

It is a GMP requirement that manufacturers control the critical aspects of their particular operations through qualification and validation over the life cycle of the product and process. Any planned changes to the facilities, equipment, utilities and processes, which may affect the quality of the product, should be formally documented and the impact on the validated status or control strategy assessed. Computerised systems used for the manufacture of medicinal products should also be validated according to the requirements of Annex 11.

Organising and Planning for Qualification and Validation:

All qualification and validation activities should be planned and take the life cycle of facilities, equipment, utilities, process and product into consideration.

Qualification and validation activities should only be performed by suitably trained personnel who follow approved procedures.

Qualification/validation personnel should report as defined in the pharmaceutical quality system although this may not necessarily be to a quality management or a quality assurance function. However, there should be appropriate quality oversight over the whole validation life cycle.

The key elements of the site qualification and validation programme should be clearly defined and documented in a validation master plan (VMP) or equivalent document.

The VMP or equivalent document should define the qualification/validation system and include or reference information on at least the following:

Qualification and Validation policy;

The organisational structure including roles and responsibilities for qualification and validation activities;

Summary of the facilities, equipment, systems, processes on site and the qualification and validation status;

Change control and deviation management for qualification and validation;

Guidance on developing acceptance criteria;

References to existing documents;

The qualification and validation strategy, including requalification, where applicable.

For large and complex projects, planning takes on added

importance and separate validation plans may enhance clarity

A quality risk management approach should be used for qualification and validation activities. In light of increased knowledge and understanding from any changes during the project phase or during commercial production, the risk assessments should be repeated, as required. The way in which risk assessments are used to support qualification and validation activities should be clearly documented.

Appropriate checks should be incorporated into qualification and validation work to ensure the integrity of all data obtained.

Documentation, Including VMP:

Good documentation practices are important to support knowledge management throughout the product lifecycle.

All documents generated during qualification and validation should be approved and authorised by appropriate personnel as defined in the pharmaceutical quality system.

The inter-relationship between documents in complex validation projects should be clearly defined.

Validation protocols should be prepared which defines the critical systems, attributes and parameters and the associated acceptance criteria.

Qualification documents may be combined together, where appropriate, e.g. installation qualification (IQ) and operational qualification (OQ).

Where validation protocols and other documentation are supplied by a third party providing validation services, appropriate personnel at the manufacturing site should confirm suitability and compliance with internal procedures before approval. Vendor protocols may be supplemented by additional documentation/test protocols before use.

Any significant changes to the approved protocol during execution, e.g. acceptance criteria, operating parameters etc., should be documented as a deviation and be scientifically justified.

Results which fail to meet the pre-defined acceptance criteria should be recorded as a deviation and be fully investigated according to local procedures. Any implications for the validation should be discussed in the report

The review and conclusions of the validation should be reported and the results obtained summarised against the acceptance criteria. Any subsequent changes to acceptance criteria should be scientifically justified and a final recommendation made as to the outcome of the validation.

A formal release for the next stage in the qualification and validation process should be authorised by the relevant responsible personnel either as part of the validation report approval or as a separate summary document. Conditional approval to proceed to the next qualification stage can be given where certain acceptance criteria or deviations have not been fully addressed and there is a documented assessment that there is no significant impact on the next activity.

Qualification Stages for Equipment's, Facilities, Utilities and Systems.

Qualification activities should consider all stages from initial development of the user requirements specification through to the end of use of the equipment, facility, utility or system. The main stages and some suggested criteria (although this depends on individual project circumstances and may be different) which could be included in each stage are indicated below:

User requirements specification (URS)

The specification for equipment, facilities, utilities or systems should be defined in a URS and/or a functional specification. The essential elements of quality need to be built in at this stage and any GMP risks mitigated to an acceptable level. The URS should be a point of reference throughout the validation life cycle.

Design qualification (DQ)

The next element in the qualification of equipment, facilities, utilities, or systems is DQ where the compliance of the design with GMP should be demonstrated and documented. The requirements of the user requirements specification should be verified during the design qualification.

Factory acceptance testing (FAT) /Site acceptance testing (SAT)

Equipment, especially if incorporating novel or complex technology, may be evaluated, if applicable, at the vendor prior to delivery.

Prior to installation, equipment should be confirmed to comply with the URS/ functional specification at the vendor site, if applicable.

Where appropriate and justified, documentation review and some tests could be performed at the FAT or other stages without the need to repeat on site at IQ/OQ if it can be shown that the functionality is not affected by the transport and installation.

FAT may be supplemented by the execution of a SAT following the receipt of equipment at the manufacturing site.

Installation qualification (IQ)

IQ should be performed on equipment, facilities, utilities, or systems.

IQ should include, but is not limited to the following:

Verification of the correct installation of components, instrumentation, equipment, pipe work and services against the engineering drawings and specifications;

Verification of the correct installation against pre-defined criteria;

Collection and collation of supplier operating and working instructions and maintenance requirements;

Calibration of instrumentation;

Verification of the materials of construction.

Operational qualification (OQ)

OQ normally follows IQ but depending on the complexity of the equipment, it may be performed as a combined Installation/Operation Qualification (IOQ).

OQ should include but is not limited to the following:

Tests that have been developed from the knowledge of processes, systems and equipment to ensure the system is operating as designed;

Tests to confirm upper and lower operating limits, and /or "worst case" conditions.

The completion of a successful OQ should allow the

finalisation of standard operating and cleaning procedures, operator training and preventative maintenance requirements.

Performance qualification (PQ)

PQ should normally follow the successful completion of IQ and OQ. However, it may in some cases be appropriate to perform it in conjunction with OQ or Process Validation.

PQ should include, but is not limited to the following:

Tests, using production materials, qualified substitutes or simulated product proven to have equivalent behaviour under normal operating conditions with worst case batch sizes. The frequency of sampling used to confirm process control should be justified;

Tests should cover the operating range of the intended process, unless documented evidence from the development phases confirming the operational ranges is available.

RE-QUALIFICATION

Equipment, facilities, utilities and systems should be evaluated at an appropriate frequency to confirm that they remain in a state of control.

Where re-qualification is necessary and performed at a specific time period, the period should be justified and the criteria for evaluation defined. Furthermore, the possibility of small changes over time should be assessed.

Process Validation

General

The requirements and principles outlined in this section are applicable to the manufacture of all pharmaceutical dosage forms. They cover the initial validation of new processes, subsequent validation of modified processes, site transfers and on-going process verification. It is implicit in this annex that a robust product development process is in place to enable successful process validation.

The guideline on Process Validation is intended to provide guidance on the information and data to be provided in the regulatory submission only. However GMP requirements for process validation continue throughout the lifecycle of the process

This approach should be applied to link product and process development. It will ensure validation of the commercial manufacturing process and maintenance of the process in a state of control during routine commercial production.

Manufacturing processes may be developed using a traditional approach or a continuous verification approach. However, irrespective of the approach used, processes must be shown to be robust and ensure consistent product quality before any product is released to the market. Manufacturing processes using the traditional approach should undergo a prospective validation programme, wherever possible, prior to certification of the product. Retrospective validation is no longer an acceptable approach.

Process validation of new products should cover all intended marketed strengths and sites of manufacture. Bracketing could be justified for new products based on extensive process knowledge from the development stage in conjunction with an appropriate on-going verification programme.

For process validation of products which are transferred

from one site to another or within the same site, the number of validation batches could be reduced by the use of a bracketing approach. However, existing product knowledge, including the content of the previous validation, should be available. Different strengths, batch sizes and pack sizes/container types may also use a bracketing approach, if justified.

For the site transfer of legacy products, the manufacturing process and controls must comply with the marketing authorisation and meet current standards for marketing authorisation for that product type. If necessary, variations to the marketing authorisation should be submitted.

Process validation should establish whether all quality attributes and process parameters, which are considered important for ensuring the validated state and acceptable product quality, can be consistently met by the process. The basis by which process parameters and quality attributes were identified as being critical or non-critical should be clearly documented, taking into account the results of any risk assessment activities.

Normally batches manufactured for process validation should be the same size as the intended commercial scale batches and the use of any other batch sizes should be justified.

Equipment, facilities, utilities and systems used for process validation should be qualified. Test methods should be validated for their intended use.

For all products irrespective of the approach used, process knowledge from development studies or other sources should be accessible to the manufacturing site, unless otherwise justified, and be the basis for validation activities.

For process validation batches, production, development, or other site transfer personnel may be involved. Batches should only be manufactured by trained personnel in accordance with GMP using approved documentation. It is expected that production personnel are involved in the manufacture of validation batches to facilitate product understanding.

The suppliers of critical starting and packaging materials should be qualified prior to the manufacture of validation batches; otherwise a justification based on the application of quality risk management principles should be documented.

It is especially important that the underlying process knowledge for the design space justification (if used) and for development of any mathematical models (if used) to confirm a process control strategy should be available.

Where validation batches are released to the market, this should be pre-defined. The conditions under which they are produced should fully comply with GMP, with the validation acceptance criteria, with any continuous process verification criteria (if used) and with the marketing authorisation or clinical trial authorisation.

Concurrent validation

In exceptional circumstances, where there is a strong benefit-risk ratio for the patient, it may be acceptable not to complete a validation programme before routine production starts and concurrent validation could be used. However, the decision to carry out concurrent validation must be justified, documented in the VMP for visibility and approved by authorised personnel.

Where a concurrent validation approach has been adopted,

there should be sufficient data to support a conclusion that any given batch of product is uniform and meets the defined acceptance criteria. The results and conclusion should be formally documented and available to the Qualified Person prior to certification of the batch.

Traditional process validation

In the traditional approach, a number of batches of the finished product are manufactured under routine conditions to confirm reproducibility.

The number of batches manufactured and the number of samples taken should be based on quality risk management principles, allow the normal range of variation and trends to be established and provide sufficient data for evaluation.

Each manufacturer must determine and justify the number of batches necessary to demonstrate a high level of assurance that the process is capable of consistently delivering quality product.

It is generally considered acceptable that a minimum of three consecutive batches manufactured under routine conditions could constitute a validation of the process. An alternative number of batches may be justified taking into account whether standard methods of manufacture are used and whether similar products or processes are already used at the site. An initial validation exercise with three batches may need to be supplemented with further data obtained from subsequent batches as part of an on-going process verification exercise.

A process validation protocol should be prepared which defines the critical process parameters (CPP), critical

quality attributes (CQA) and the associated acceptance
criteria which should be based on development data or
documented process knowledge.

Process validation protocols should include, but are not
limited to the following:
A short description of the process and a reference to the
respective Master Batch Record;
Functions and responsibilities;
Summary of the CQAs to be investigated;
Summary of CPPs and their associated limits;
Summary of other (non-critical) attributes and parameters
which will be investigated or monitored during the
validation activity, and the reasons for their inclusion;
List of the equipment/facilities to be used (including
measuring/monitoring/recording equipment) together
with the calibration status;
List of analytical methods and method validation, as
appropriate.
Proposed in-process controls with acceptance criteria and
the reason(s) why each in-process control is selected;

Additional testing to be carried out with acceptance
criteria;
Sampling plan and the rationale behind it;
Methods for recording and evaluating results;
Process for release and certification of batches (if
applicable).

Continuous process verification
For products developed by a quality by design approach,
where it has been scientifically established during

development that the established control strategy provides a high degree of assurance of product quality, then continuous process verification can be used as an alternative to traditional process validation.

The method by which the process will be verified should be defined. There should be a science based control strategy for the required attributes for incoming materials, critical quality attributes and critical process parameters to confirm product realisation. This should also include regular evaluation of the control strategy. Process Analytical Technology and multivariate statistical process control may be used as tools. Each manufacturer must determine and justify the number of batches necessary to demonstrate a high level of assurance that the process is capable of consistently delivering quality product.

Hybrid approach

A hybrid of the traditional approach and continuous process verification could be used where there is a substantial amount of product and process knowledge and understanding which has been gained from manufacturing experience and historical batch data.

This approach may also be used for any validation activities after changes or during on-going process verification even though the product was initially validated using a traditional approach.

Ongoing Process Verification during Lifecycle

On-going process applicable to all three approaches to process validation mentioned above, i.e. traditional, continuous and hybrid.

Manufacturers should monitor product quality to ensure

that a state of control is maintained throughout the product lifecycle with the relevant process trends

The extent and frequency of on-going process verification should be reviewed periodically. At any point throughout the product lifecycle, it may be appropriate to modify the requirements taking into account the current level of process understanding and process performance.

On-going process verification should be conducted under an approved protocol or equivalent documents and a corresponding report should be prepared to document the results obtained. Statistical tools should be used, where appropriate, to support any conclusions with regard to the variability and capability of a given process and ensure a state of control.

On-going process verification should be used throughout the product lifecycle to support the validated status of the product as documented in the Product Quality Review. Incremental changes over time should also be considered and the need for any additional actions, e.g. enhanced sampling, should be assessed.

Verification of Transportation

Finished medicinal products, investigational medicinal products, bulk product and samples should be transported from manufacturing sites in accordance with the conditions defined in the marketing authorisation, the approved label, product specification file or as justified by the manufacturer.

It is recognised that verification of transportation may be challenging due to the variable factors involved however, transportation routes should be clearly defined. Seasonal and other variations should also be considered during verification of transport

A risk assessment should be performed to consider the impact of variables in the transportation process other than those conditions which are continuously controlled or monitored, e.g. delays during transportation, failure of monitoring devices, topping up liquid nitrogen, product susceptibility and any other relevant factors.

Due to the variable conditions expected during transportation, continuous monitoring and recording of any critical environmental conditions to which the product may be subjected should be performed, unless otherwise justified.

Validation of Packing

Variation in equipment processing parameters especially during primary packaging may have a significant impact on the integrity and correct functioning of the pack, e.g. blister strips, sachets and sterile components, therefore primary and secondary packaging equipment for finished and bulk products should be qualified.

Qualification of the equipment used for primary packing should be carried out at the minimum and maximum operating ranges defined for the critical process parameters such as temperature, machine speed and sealing pressure or for any other factors.

Qualification of Utilities

The quality of steam, water, air, other gases etc. should be confirmed following installation using the qualification steps.

The period and extent of qualification should reflect any seasonal variations, if applicable, and the intended use of the utility.

A risk assessment should be carried out where there may be direct contact with the product, e.g. heating, ventilation and air-conditioning (HVAC) systems, or indirect contact such as through heat exchangers to mitigate any risks of failure.

Validation of Test Methods

All analytical test methods used in qualification, validation or cleaning exercises should be validated with an appropriate detection and quantification limit.

Where microbial testing of product is carried out, the method should be validated to confirm that the product does not influence the recovery of microorganisms.

Where microbial testing of surfaces in clean rooms is carried out, validation should be performed on the test method to confirm that sanitizing agents do not influence the recovery of microorganisms.

Cleaning Validation

Cleaning validation should be performed in order to confirm the effectiveness of any cleaning procedure for all product contact equipment. Simulating agents may be used with appropriate scientific justification. Where similar types of equipment are grouped together, a justification of the specific equipment selected for cleaning validation is expected.

A visual check for cleanliness is an important part of the acceptance criteria for cleaning validation.

It is recognised that a cleaning validation programme may take some time to complete and validation with verification after each batch may be required for some products, e.g. investigational medicinal products. There should be sufficient data from the verification to support a conclusion that the equipment is clean and available for further use.

Validation should consider the level of automation in the cleaning process. Where an automatic process is used, the specified normal operating range of the utilities and equipment should be validated.

For all cleaning processes an assessment should be performed to determine the variable factors which influence cleaning effectiveness and performance, e.g. operators, the level of detail in procedures such as rinsing times etc. If variable factors have been identified, the worst case situations should be used as the basis for cleaning validation studies.

Limits for the carryover of product residues should be based on a toxicological evaluation. The justification for the selected limits should be documented in a risk assessment which includes all the supporting references. Limits should be established for the removal of any cleaning agents used. Acceptance criteria should consider the potential cumulative effect of multiple items of equipment in the process equipment train.

If it is not feasible to test for specific product residues, other representative parameters may be selected, e.g. total organic carbon (TOC) and conductivity.

The risk presented by microbial and endotoxin contamination should be considered during the development of cleaning validation protocols.

The influence of the time between manufacture and cleaning and the time between cleaning and use should be taken into account to define dirty and clean hold times for the cleaning process.

Where campaign manufacture is carried out, the impact on the ease of cleaning at the end of the campaign should be considered and the maximum length of a campaign (in time and/or number of batches) should be the basis for cleaning validation exercises.

Where a worst case product approach is used as a cleaning validation model, a scientific rationale should be provided for the selection of the worst case product and the impact of new products to the site assessed. Criteria for determining the worst case may include solubility, cleanability, toxicity and potency.

Cleaning validation protocols should specify or reference the locations to be sampled, the rationale for the selection of these locations and define the acceptance criteria.

Sampling should be carried out by swabbing and/or rinsing or by other means depending on the production equipment. The sampling materials and method should not influence the result. Recovery should be shown to be possible from all product contact materials sampled in the equipment with all the sampling methods used.

The cleaning procedure should be performed an appropriate number of times based on a risk assessment and meet the acceptance criteria in order to prove that the cleaning method is validated.

Where a cleaning process is ineffective or is not appropriate for some equipment, dedicated equipment or other appropriate measures should be used for each product.

Where manual cleaning of equipment is performed, it is especially important that the effectiveness of the manual process should be confirmed at a justified frequency.

Definitions

Definitions of terms relating to qualification and validation which are not given in other sections of the current EudraLex, Volume 4, are given below.

Bracketing approach.

A science and risk based validation approach such that only batches on the extremes of certain predetermined and justified design factors, e.g. strength, batch size and/or pack size, are tested during process validation. The design assumes that validation of any intermediate levels is represented by validation of the extremes. Where a range of strengths is to be validated, bracketing could be applicable if the strengths are identical or very closely related in composition, e.g. for a tablet range made with different compression weights of a similar basic granulation or a capsule range made by filling different plug fill weights of the same basic composition into different size capsule shells. Bracketing can be applied to different container sizes or different fills in the same container closure system.

Change Control.

A formal system by which qualified representatives of appropriate disciplines review proposed or actual changes that might affect the validated status of facilities, systems, equipment or processes. The intent is to determine the need for action to ensure and document that the system is maintained in a validated state.

Cleaning Validation.

Cleaning validation is documented evidence that an approved cleaning procedure will reproducibly remove the previous product or cleaning agents used in the equipment below the scientifically set maximum allowable carryover level.

Cleaning verification.

The gathering of evidence through chemical analysis after each batch/campaign to show that the residues of the previous product or cleaning agents have been reduced below the scientifically set maximum allowable carryover level.

Concurrent Validation.

Validation carried out in exceptional circumstances, justified on the basis of significant patient benefit, where the validation protocol is executed concurrently with commercialisation of the validation batches.

Continuous process verification.

An alternative approach to process validation in which manufacturing process performance is continuously monitored and evaluated. (ICH Q8)

Critical process parameter (CPP).

A process parameter whose variability has an impact on a critical quality attribute and therefore should be monitored or controlled to ensure the process produces the desired quality. (ICH Q8)

Critical quality attribute (CQA).

A physical, chemical, biological or microbiological property or characteristic that should be within an approved limit, range or distribution to ensure the desired product quality. (ICH Q8)

Design qualification (DQ).

The documented verification that the proposed design of the facilities, systems and equipment is suitable for the intended purpose.

Installation Qualification (IQ).

The documented verification that the facilities, systems and equipment, as installed or modified, comply with the approved design and the manufacturer's recommendations.

Lifecycle.

All phases in the life of a product, equipment or facility from initial development or use through to discontinuation of use.

Ongoing Process Verification (also known as continued process verification).

Documented evidence that the process remains in a state of control during commercial manufacture.

Operational Qualification (OQ).

The documented verification that the facilities, systems and equipment, as installed or modified, perform as intended throughout the anticipated operating ranges.

Performance Qualification (PQ).

The documented verification that systems and equipment can perform effectively and reproducibly based on the approved process method and product specification.

Process Validation.

The documented evidence that the process, operated within established parameters, can perform effectively and reproducibly to produce a medicinal product meeting its predetermined specifications and quality attributes.

Prospective Validation.

Validation carried out before routine production of products intended for sale.

Quality by design.

A systematic approach that begins with predefined objectives and emphasises product and process understanding and process control, based on sound science and quality risk management.

Quality risk management.

A systematic process for the assessment, control, communication and review of risks to quality across the lifecycle.

State of control.

A condition in which the set of controls consistently provides assurance of acceptable process performance and product quality.

Traditional approach.

A product development approach where set points and operating ranges for process parameters are defined to ensure reproducibility.

Worst Case.

A condition or set of conditions encompassing upper and lower processing limits and circumstances, within standard operating procedures, which pose the greatest chance of product or process failure when compared to ideal conditions. Such conditions do not necessarily induce product or process failure.

User requirements Specification (URS).

The set of owner, user and engineering requirements necessary and sufficient to create a feasible design meeting the intended purpose of the system.

Module-8 Pharmaceutical Quality Management system (QMS) Requirements as Per GMP

What is QMS?

QMS is a structured collection of policies, processes, documented procedures and records and their associated responsibilities. QMS System includes Change control,

Deviation, Corrective and Preventive action, Investigation, Market Compliant, Out of Specification (OOS).

What are the benefits of QMS?

It Simplify, Clarify and Control the system

Simplify

Structured and written policies, processes and procedures

Opportunities to review and help the organization become more competitive

 Improved communication within the organization

Structured approaches in correcting defects, mistakes or deviations

CAPA are consistently undertaken based on priority and risk

CAPA process ensures higher risk problems and issues are promptly and properly

Improved complaint handling results to better customer satisfaction

Clarify

QMS clarifies roles and responsibilities

QMS helps understand the internal processes and how these processes link together

Employees understand where their contribution fits in the big picture

QMS will drive consistency in the various processes, as well as, continuous improvement.

Control

Control processes for better effectiveness and to increase efficiency

Measure, monitor and encourage continuous improvement

in quality and productivity which will become part of the organization culture Involvement of top management

Regular measurement, training and reporting to executive management of critical indicators

Pharmaceutical Quality System

Quality Management is a wide-ranging concept, which covers all matters, which individually or collectively influence the quality of a product. It is the sum total of the organised arrangements made with the objective of ensuring that medicinal products are of the quality required for their intended use. Quality Management therefore incorporates Good Manufacturing Practice.

GMP applies to the lifecycle stages from the manufacture of investigational medicinal products, technology transfer, commercial manufacturing through to product discontinuation.

The size and complexity of the company's activities should be taken into consideration when developing a new Pharmaceutical Quality System or modifying an existing one. The design of the system should incorporate appropriate risk management principles including the use of appropriate tools. While some aspects of the system can be company-wide and others site-specific, the effectiveness of the system is normally demonstrated at the site level.

A Pharmaceutical Quality System appropriate for the manufacture of medicinal products should ensure that:

Product realisation is achieved by designing, planning, implementing, maintaining and continuously improving a system that allows the consistent delivery of products with appropriate quality attributes;

Product and process knowledge is managed throughout all

lifecycle stages;

Medicinal products are designed and developed in a way that takes account of the requirements of Good Manufacturing Practice;

Production and control operations are clearly specified and Good Manufacturing Practice adopted;

Managerial responsibilities are clearly specified;

Arrangements are made for the manufacture, supply and use of the correct starting and packaging materials, the selection and monitoring of suppliers and for verifying that each delivery is from the approved supply chain;

Processes are in place to assure the management of outsourced activities.

A state of control is established and maintained by developing and using effective monitoring and control systems for process performance and product quality.

The results of product and processes monitoring are taken into account in batch release, in the investigation of deviations, and, with a view to taking preventive action to avoid potential deviations occurring in the future.

All necessary controls on intermediate products, and any other in-process controls and validations are carried out;

Continual improvement is facilitated through the implementation of quality improvements appropriate to the current level of process and product knowledge.

Arrangements are in place for the prospective evaluation of planned changes and their approval prior to implementation taking into account regulatory notification and approval where required;

After implementation of any change, an evaluation is undertaken to confirm the quality objectives were achieved and that there was no unintended deleterious impact on product quality;

An appropriate level of root cause analysis should be applied during the investigation of deviations, suspected product defects and other problems. This can be determined using Quality Risk Management principles.

Medicinal products are not sold or supplied before a Qualified Person has certified that each production batch has been produced and controlled in accordance with the requirements of the Marketing Authorisation and any other regulations relevant to the production, control and release of medicinal products;

Satisfactory arrangements exist to ensure, as far as possible, that the medicinal products are stored, distributed and subsequently handled so that quality is maintained throughout their shelf life;

There is a process for self-inspection and/or quality audit, which regularly appraises the effectiveness and applicability of the Pharmaceutical Quality System.

Senior management has the ultimate responsibility to ensure an effective Pharmaceutical Quality System is in place, adequately resourced and that roles, responsibilities, and authorities are defined, communicated and implemented throughout the organisation. Senior management's leadership and active participation in the Pharmaceutical Quality System is essential. This leadership should ensure the support and commitment of staff at all levels and sites within the organisation to the Pharmaceutical Quality System.

There should be periodic management review, with the involvement of senior management, of the operation of the Pharmaceutical Quality System to identify opportunities for continual improvement of products, processes and the system itself.

The Pharmaceutical Quality System should be defined and documented. A Quality Manual or equivalent documentation should be established and should contain a description of the quality management system including management responsibilities.

Good Manufacturing Practice for Medicinal Products

Good Manufacturing Practice is that part of Quality Management which ensures that products are consistently produced and controlled to the quality standards appropriate to their intended use and as required by the Marketing Authorisation, Clinical Trial Authorisation or product specification. Good Manufacturing Practice is concerned with both production and quality control. The basic requirements of GMP are that:

(i) All manufacturing processes are clearly defined, systematically reviewed in the light of experience and shown to be capable of consistently manufacturing medicinal products of the required quality and complying with their specifications;

(ii) Critical steps of manufacturing processes and significant changes to the Process are validated;

(iii) All necessary facilities for GMP are provided including:

Appropriately qualified and trained personnel;

Adequate premises and space;

Suitable equipment and services;

Correct materials, containers and labels;

Approved procedures and instructions, in accordance with the Pharmaceutical Quality System;

Suitable storage and transport;

(iv) Instructions and procedures are written in an instructional form in clear and unambiguous (it is clear and cannot be understood wrongly) language, specifically applicable to the facilities provided;

(v) Procedures are carried out correctly and operators are trained to do so;

(vi) Records are made, manually and/or by recording instruments, during manufacture which demonstrate that all the steps required by the defined procedures and instructions were in fact taken and that the quantity and quality of the product was as expected.

(vii) Any significant deviations are fully recorded, investigated with the objective of determining the root cause and appropriate corrective and preventive action implemented;

(viii) Records of manufacture including distribution which enable the complete history of a batch to be traced are retained in a comprehensible and accessible form;

(ix) The distribution of the products minimises any risk to their quality and takes account of Good Distribution Practice;

(x) A system is available to recall any batch of product, from sale or supply;

(xi) Complaints about products are examined, the causes of quality defects investigated and appropriate measures taken in respect of the defective products and to prevent reoccurrence.

Product Quality Review

Regular periodic or rolling quality reviews of all authorised medicinal products, including export only products, should be conducted with the objective of verifying the consistency of the existing process, the appropriateness of current specifications for both starting materials and finished product, to highlight any trends and to identify product and process improvements.

Such reviews should normally be conducted and documented annually, taking into account previous reviews, and should include at least:

(i) A review of starting materials including packaging materials used in the Product, especially those from new sources and in particular the review of supply chain traceability of active substances.

(ii) A review of all batches that failed to meet established specification(s) and their investigation.

(iii) A review of all significant deviations or non-conformances, their related Investigations and the effectiveness of resultant corrective and preventive Actions taken.

(iv) A review of all changes carried out to the processes or analytical methods.

(v) A review of Marketing Authorisation variations submitted, granted or Refused, including those for third country (export only) dossiers.

(vi) A review of the results of the stability monitoring programme and any Adverse trends.

(vii) A review of all quality-related returns, complaints and recalls and the Investigations performed at the time.

(viii) A review of adequacy of any other previous product process or equipment corrective actions

(ix) For new marketing authorizations and variations to marketing authorizations, a review of post marketing commitments

(x) The qualification status of relevant equipment and utilities, e.g. HVAC, water, compressed gases, etc.

The Management As per US FDA guideline:

Many of the modern quality system concepts described here correlate very closely with the CGMP regulations (refer to the charts later in the document). Current industry practice generally divides the responsibilities of the quality control unit (QCU), as defined in the CGMP regulations, between quality control (QC) and quality assurance (QA) functions.

QC usually involves

(1) Assessing the suitability of incoming components, containers, closures, labeling, in-process materials, and the finished products;
(2) Evaluating the performance of the manufacturing process to ensure adherence to proper specifications and limits; and
(3) Determining the acceptability of each batch for release.

QA primarily involves

(1) Review and approval of all procedures related to production and maintenance,
(2) review of associated records, and
(3) Auditing and performing/evaluating trend analyses

Under a quality system, it is normally expected that the product and process development units, the manufacturing units, and the QU will remain independent. In very limited circumstances, a single individual can perform both production and quality functions. That person is still accountable for implementing all the controls and reviewing the results of manufacture to ensure that product quality standards have been met. Under such circumstances, it is recommended that another qualified individual, not involved in the production operation, conduct an additional, periodic review of QU activities.

Quality System as per GMP Guideline

The FDA's Drug Manufacturing Inspection Compliance Program, which contains instructions to FDA personnel for conducting inspections, is a systems-based approach to inspection and is very consistent with the robust quality system model presented in this guidance.

The diagram below shows the relationship among the six systems: the quality system and the five manufacturing systems. The quality system provides the foundation for the manufacturing systems that are linked and function within it.

The quality system model described in this guidance does not consider the five manufacturing systems as discrete entities, but instead integrates them into appropriate sections of the model.

Those familiar with the six-system inspection approach will see organizational differences in this guidance; however, the inter-relationship should be readily apparent.

One of the important themes of the systems based inspection compliance program is that you have the ability to assess whether each of the systems is in a state of control. The quality system model presented in this guidance will also serve to help firms achieve this state of control.

Module-9 Pharmaceutical Plant Self-Inspection, Quality audits and Suppliers' Audit Requirements as Per GMP

What is Self Inspection :

Self Inspection or Internal Audit is a Quality System to check whether activities followed by all departments are according to the written approved procedures and complying with the cGMP and Regulatory Requirements.

What are the Objective of Self Inspection :

Promote awareness for Quality and CGMP within plant

Proactive approach to identify and correct the non-conformance

Assure the effectiveness and support continuous improvement of compliance to CGMP and Quality management system.

Develop confidence to minimize and possibly to eliminate the scope for major or critical regulatory findings.

To identify the non-compliance or Gap with respect to Manufacturing Practices of production, Quality Control systems, quality assurance procedures, engineering practices, environmental conditions etc.

The purpose of self-inspection is to evaluate the manufacturers or the plants compliance with GMP in all aspects of production, Quality assurance and Quality Control.

The self-inspection programme should be designed to detect any shortcomings in the implementation of GMP and to recommend the necessary corrective actions. Self-inspections should be performed routinely and may be in addition, performed on special occasions, e.g. in the case of product recalls or repeated rejections, or when an inspection by the health authorities is announced. The team responsible for self-inspection should consist of personnel who can evaluate the implementation of GMP All recommendations for corrective action should be implemented.

The procedure for self-inspection should be documented, and there should be an effective follow-up programme.

Written instructions for self-inspection should be established to provide a minimum and uniform standard of requirements. These may include questionnaires on GMP requirements covering at least the following items:

(a) Personnel;

(b) Premises including personnel facilities;

(c) Maintenance of buildings and equipment;

(d) Storage of starting materials and finished products;

(e) Equipment and instruments

(f) Production and in-process controls;

(g) Quality control

(h) Documentation;

(i) Sanitation and hygiene;

(j) Validation and revalidation programmes;

(k) Calibration of instruments or measurement systems;

(l) Recall procedures;

(m) Complaints management;

(n) Results of previous self-inspections and any corrective steps taken.

Self-inspection Team :

Management should appoint a self-inspection team consisting of experts in their respective fields who are familiar with GMP. The members of the team may be appointed from inside or outside the company.

Frequency of self-inspection :
The frequency with which self-inspections are conducted
may depend on company requirements but should
preferably be at least once a year. The frequency should be
stated in the procedure.

Self-inspection Reports :
A report should be made at the completion of a self-
inspection. The report should include:
(a) Self-inspection results;
(b) Evaluation and conclusions;
(c) Recommended corrective actions.
There should be an effective follow-up programme. The
company management should evaluate both the self-
inspection report and the corrective actions as necessary.

Quality Audits :
It may be useful to supplement self-inspections with a
quality audit. A quality audit consists of an examination
and assessment of all or part of a quality system with the
specific purpose of improving it. A quality audit is usually
conducted by outside or independent specialists or a team
designated by the management for this purpose. Such
audits may also be extended to suppliers and contractors.
The contract giver shall performed audit at contract
acceptors site periodically or before giving contract for
manufacturing of products.

Suppliers' audits and Approval :
The person responsible for QA or CQA should have

responsibility, together with other relevant departments, for approving suppliers who can reliably supply Raw and packaging materials that meet established specifications.

Before suppliers are approved and included in the approved suppliers' list or specifications, they should be evaluated. The evaluation should take into account a supplier's history and the nature of the materials to be supplied.

If an audit is required, it should determine the supplier's ability to conform with GMP standards.

Module-10 Pharmaceutical Plant Complaints and Product Recall as Per GMP

Complaints :

What is Product Complaints:

Any Manufacturing or Packaging related complaints with respect to a Product, including (a) any complaint involving the possible failure of Product to meet any of the specifications or (b) any dissatisfaction or unhappiness with the design, package or labeling of such Product. Complaints come to the manufacturer after selling of product to the market.

All complaints and other information concerning potentially defective products should be carefully reviewed according to written procedures and the corrective action should be taken.

A person responsible for handling the complaints and deciding the measures to be taken should be allocated, together with sufficient supporting staff to assist him or her.

There should be written procedures describing the action

to be taken, including the need to consider a recall, in the case of a complaint concerning a possible product defect.

Special attention should be given to establishing that the product that gave rise to a complaint was defective.

Any complaint concerning a product defect should be recorded with all the original details and thoroughly investigated. The person responsible for Quality Assurance should normally be involved in the review of such investigations.

If a product defect is discovered or suspected in a batch, consideration should be given to whether other batches should be checked in order to determine whether they are also affected. In particular, other batches that may contain reprocessed product from the defective batch should be investigated.

Where necessary, appropriate follow-up action, possibly including product recall, should be taken after investigation and evaluation of the complaint.

All decisions made and measures taken as a result of a complaint should be recorded and referenced to the corresponding batch records.

Complaints records should be regularly reviewed for any indication of specific or repeating problems that require attention and might justify the recall of marketed products.

The competent authorities should be informed if a manufacturer is considering action following possibly faulty manufacture, product deterioration, a suspect product or any other serious quality problems with a product.

Product Recalls :

What is Product Recall :

A product recall is a request from a manufacturer or

company to return or removal of a marketed product after the discovery of safety issues or product defects that might threaten the consumer or put the company/seller/manufacturer at risk of legal action.

There should be a system to recall the products from the market, promptly and effectively, products known or suspected to be defective.

The authorized person should be responsible for the execution and coordination of recalls. He or she should have sufficient staff to handle all aspects of the recalls with the appropriate degree of urgency.

There should be established written procedures, which are regularly reviewed and updated, for the organization of any recall activity. Recall operations should be capable of being initiated promptly down to the required level in the distribution chain.

An instruction should be included in the written procedures to store recalled products in a secure segregated area while their fate is decided.

All competent authorities of all countries to which a given product has been distributed should be promptly informed of any intention to recall the product because it is, or is suspected of being, defective.

The distribution records should be readily available to the authorized person, and they should contain sufficient information on wholesalers and directly supplied customers (including, for exported products, those who have received samples for clinical tests and medical samples) to permit an effective recall.

The progress of the recall process should be monitored and recorded.

Records should include the disposition of the product and

final report should be issued, including reconciliation between the delivered and recovered quantities of the products.

The effectiveness of the arrangements for recalls should be tested and evaluated from time to time.

Mock recall to be performed at a regular interval to check the effectiveness of the recall.

What is Recall of Product :

A product recall is a request from a manufacturer to return or removal of a marketed product after the discovery of safety issues or product defects that might endanger the consumer or put the maker/seller/ manufacturer at risk of legal action.

The manufacturer not only has to pay the cost of replacing & fixing of defective products but also it will down the image of Organization.

There are different types of recall i.e. Class I, Class II & Class III.

Class I :

A Recall situation in which there is a reasonable probability that the use of, or exposure to, a defective product is life threatening or could cause serious risk to health or death. Recall and procedure to be initiated within 24 hrs.

Class II :

A Recall situation in which the use of, or exposure to, a defective product could cause illness or mistreatment but is not Class- I. Recall and procedure to be initiated within 48 hrs.

Class III :

A Recall situation in which the use of, or exposure to, a

defective product is not Class - I or Class - II and may not pose a significant hazard to health, but withdrawal may have been initiated for other reasons.

To be recalled after hearing and answering show cause notice.

What is the meaning of Mock :

Make a Duplicate or exact copy of something

What is Mock recall:

Mock recalls are routine exercises conducted by manufacturers, processors, distributors and other various trading partners in the supply chain to assess or verify their recall procedures and responsiveness and to train the recall team.

Mock recall has to confirm the efficient collation of batch history details and effectiveness of communication channels.

Module-11 Pharmaceutical Plant Contract Manufacturing and Contract Analysis as Per GMP
The Contract Analysis :
What is Contract :

The definition of a contract is an agreement between two or more people to do something. Example suppose X company is manufacturing some products for Y Company so here X Company is called Contract Acceptor and Y Company is called as Contract giver.

Contract should describe clearly who is responsible for purchasing materials, testing & releasing them, undertaking production & quality controls including the in-process control and who has responsibility for samples & analysis.

There must be a written contract between the contract giver and the contract acceptor which clearly establishes the responsibilities of each party, covering the outsourced activities, the products or operations to which they are related, communication processes relating to the outsourced activities and any technical arrangements made in connection with it.

The contract must clearly state the way in which the authorized person, in releasing each batch of product for sale or issuing the certificate of analysis, exercises his or her full responsibility and ensures that each batch has been manufactured in, and checked for, compliance with the requirements of the marketing authorization.

Technical aspects of the contract should be drawn up by competent persons with suitable knowledge of pharmaceutical technology, analysis and GMP.

All arrangements for production and analysis must be in accordance with the marketing authorization and agreed by both parties.

The contract should clearly describe who is responsible for contracted activities, e.g. knowledge management, technology transfer, supply chain, subcontracting, testing and releasing materials and undertaking production and QC, including in-process controls, and who has responsibility for sampling and analysis.

Manufacturing, analytical and distribution records, and reference samples, should be kept by, or be available to, the contract giver. Any records relevant to assessing the quality of a product in the event of complaints or a suspected defect, or to investigating in the case of a suspected falsified product or laboratory fraud, must be accessible and specified in the procedures of the contract giver.

The contract should describe the handling of starting materials, intermediate, bulk and finished products, if they are rejected. It should also describe the procedure to be followed if the contract analysis shows that the tested product must be rejected.

General Requirements :

Contract production, analysis and any other activity covered by GMP must be correctly defined, agreed and controlled in order to avoid misunderstandings that could result in a product, or analysis, of unsatisfactory quality.

All arrangements for contract production and analysis, including technology transfer and any proposed changes in technical or other arrangements, should be in accordance with the marketing authorization for the product concerned.

The contract should permit the contract giver to audit the facilities and activities of the contract acceptor or mutually agreed subcontractors.

In the case of contract analysis, the final approval for release must be given by the authorized person in accordance with GMP and the marketing authorization as specified in the contract.

Responsibilities of contract Giver :

Before giving contract to a company or organization the contract giver shall perform audit which includes the premises, Facility, Equipment's, System etc. and after satisfactory outcome the contract giver has to give the contract to the respective company or the contract acceptor for manufacturing of products.

The Pharmaceutical Quality System of the contract giver should include the control and review of any outsourced activities.

The contract giver is responsible for assessing the legality, suitability and competence of the contract acceptor to successfully carry out the work or tests required, for approval for contract activities, and for ensuring by means of the contract that the principles of GMP are followed.

The contract giver should provide the contract acceptor with all the information necessary to carry out the operations correctly in accordance with the marketing authorization and any other legal requirements. The contract giver should ensure that the contract acceptor is fully aware of any hazards associated with the product, work or tests that might pose a risk to premises, equipment, personnel, other materials or other products.

The contract giver should review and assess the records and results related to the outsourced activities. The contract giver should ensure that all products and materials delivered by the contract acceptor have been processed in accordance with GMP and the marketing authorization; comply with their specifications and that the product has been released by the authorized person in accordance with GMP and the marketing authorization.

The contract giver should monitor and review the performance of the contract acceptor including the implementation of any needed improvements and their effectiveness.

The contract giver is responsible for ensuring that the contract acceptor understands that his or her activities may be subject to inspection by competent authorities.

Responsibilities of Contract Acceptor :

The contract acceptor must have adequate premises, equipment, knowledge, experience and competent personnel to satisfactorily carry out the work ordered by the contract giver.

Contract manufacture may be undertaken only by a manufacturer who holds a valid manufacturing authorization.

The contract acceptor should not pass to a third party any of the work entrusted to him or her under the contract without the contract giver's prior evaluation and approval of the arrangements.

Arrangements made between the contract acceptor and any third party should ensure that information and knowledge, including that from assessments of the suitability of the third party, are made available in the same way as between the original contract giver and contract acceptor

The contract acceptor should refrain from any activity (including unauthorized changes outside the terms of the contract) that may adversely affect the quality of the product manufactured and/or analyzed for the contract giver.

www.ingramcontent.com/pod-product-compliance
Lightning Source LLC
LaVergne TN
LVHW050418160726
843469LV00041B/1134